Titi Wants a New Tutu

First Edition

There is no greater agony than bearing an untold story inside you–Maya Angelou

There once was a lovely little dancer named Titi. Her dream was to become one of the world's greatest ballerinas. She was bold and determined. She knew she could do it!

BALLET FUELLED A SPARK IN
HER SPIRIT. SHE NEVER
MISSED A REHEARSAL OR
PERFORMANCE. SHE WAS A
GREAT DANCER, TURNING
HEADS AT EVERY SHOW.

BUT THERE WAS
SOMETHING MISSING.
SHE WAS TIRED OF
WEARING THE SAME OLD
TUTUS!

Each time she danced, her Mama would dress her up in the same pair of white tights, a beige tutu, and matching ballet shoes.

'MAMA, I'M TIRED OF WEARING THE SAME THING. THE COLOURS DON'T EVEN MATCH,' SHE SAID AFTER REHEARSAL ONE DAY.

'SORRY, HONEY, THIS IS WHAT I CAN AFFORD,' MAMA SAID.

Titi tugged at the bottom of her dress and folded her arms. She frowned so hard there were lines on her forehead too.

'now Behave yourself!' Mama scolded. 'let's go home and rest. Your big dance is in two days.'

Mama held her hand as She stomped her feet on their way home.

The next day, Titi woke up with a smile from ear to ear. It was a bright
Saturday, and she had a great idea!

She sat up on the bed and looked
at the posters of classic ballet dancers on the
walls of her room.

She said her prayers and brushed
her teeth before heading
downstairs.

MAMA HAD ALREADY STARTED MAKING BREAKFAST. SHE COULD SMELL HER FAVOURITE.

TOAST, EGGS, AND BAKED BEANS. YUMMY!

After her meal with Mama and Papa, she tiptoed to the storeroom, when no one was watching.

THE STOREROOM HAD A TINY OLD SEWING
MACHINE AND LOTS OF FABRIC. IT WAS
SPLENDID.

THERE WERE SEQUINS,
DIFFERENT-SHAPED
BUTTONS, LACES,
SPARKLES, GLITTER AND
MANY, MANY LAYERS OF
FABRIC.

This was just what she needed to put her idea into action! She would create her own ballet outfit if she didn't like what Mama made her wear.

Her big brown eyes kept getting bigger and bigger as she walked into the middle of the room. The colours were very pretty.

Titi looked through the fabrics, picking out the colours she liked. She smiled widely as she looked at all the shades. It was like the rainbow had appeared in the room—red, orange, yellow, green, blue, indigo, and violet!

'Titi? Titi?' Mama called from downstairs.
There was no answer.
Mama checked Titi's room, but she wasn't
there.

She heard sounds from the storeroom and
decided to check in there. She popped her
head inside.

AND THERE TITI WAS, LYING ON THE MOUNTAIN OF FABRICS, HER CURLY AFRO TANGLED UP IN A BALL OF YARN AND STRIPS OF MATERIAL.

SHE GIGGLED IN DELIGHT.

'You've made a mess!' Mama chimed.

'Sorry Mama. I just want to make my own magical ballerina dress for the grand show tomorrow!' Titi replied.

Mama shook her head. Titi just wouldn't take no for an answer. Mama helped untangle Titi's Afro, and chose the loveliest of fabrics.

'All right, come on then, let's get to work!' Mama said.

Titi sat next to her, looking on delighted. She imagined how she would look in her new ballet outfit.

Mama spun and spun the sewing machine. It was like magic!

'Can I please hold the box of tools, Mama?' The box had pointy needles and scissors.

'No, darling, it could hurt you.' Mama moved it to the top shelf, where Titi couldn't reach.

'Awww, can I hold the ends of the dress then, please?'

Mama nodded. She showed Titi how to gather and straighten the seams as they fell to the floor.

Finally, the last seam was done. Mama held the dress up. Titi grabbed it and pulled it over her head to try it on.

It was truly beautiful!

Thanks, Mama! I love it!'

Titi jumped up and down in excitement.
The dress was just perfect.

'I want to go show Papa,' Titi said.

She hopped across the
hallway to where he sat,
and swayed this way and
that for Papa to see.

Papa gave her a thumbs-up.
'Truly magical! You'll be
the best dressed ballerina
tomorrow.'

The next day, Titi woke up very early for the performance. She went over her dance routine for the hundredth time to make it perfect.

Mama helped her get ready. Everything was just right: her hair, her dress, and her shoes. She looked very pretty in her enchanting outfit.

When they were all ready, Papa drove them to the school auditorium where the grand ballet performance of the year was taking place.

All heads turned when Titi walked on stage.
In her beautiful dress, she stood out among
the rest of the ballerinas.

She started out dancing nervously. But after Mama and Papa got up to cheer, she gained her confidence back.

Plier, Étendre, Relever, Glisser, Sauter, Élancer, Tourner
Plier, Étendre, Relever, Glisser, Sauter, Élancer, Tourner
Titi danced.

After her last step and bow, the crowd got up to give her a standing ovation.

The dress had not only made her even prettier, but it had also given her great luck for the grand performance!

TITI'S DREAM OF BECOMING THE WORLD'S GREATEST BALLERINA

HAD COME TRUE!

Acknowledgements

Thanks to the Almighty God for this great blessing!

Special thanks to my amazing parents, for teaching me that I could do anything I put my mind to. To Papaa, for all our wonderful conversations about art and literature, and for constantly motivating me to publish my first book. I finally did it! To Mum for all your sacrifice.

To my ever supportive husband. Thanks for listening to all of my ideas. I appreciate the late nights you helped me out and for your hands-on support throughout this entire journey. We made it.

And to my siblings for cheering me on.

Milton Keynes UK
Ingram Content Group UK Ltd.
UKHW050239210923
429087UK00002B/12